# A DORLING KINDERSLEY BOOK

**Written by** Angela Royston
**Photography by** Tim Ridley
**Illustrations by** Jane Cradock-Watson and Dave Hopkins
**Car consultant and model maker** Ted Taylor

Aladdin Books
Macmillan Publishing Company
866 Third Avenue
New York, NY 10022

Eye Openers ™
First published in Great Britain in 1991
by Dorling Kindersley Limited,
9 Henrietta Street, London WC2E 8PS

Reproduced by Colourscan, Singapore
Printed and bound in Italy by L.E.G.O., Vicenza

1 2 3 4 5 6 7 8 9 10

ISBN 0-689-71517-X

Library of Congress CIP data is available.

# ·EYE·OPENERS·

# Cars

ALADDIN BOOKS
MACMILLAN PUBLISHING COMPANY
NEW YORK

# Hatchback

This small car is a hatchback. The back door lifts up. Inside there is lots of room for shopping bags. Hatchbacks are quick and easy to drive. They get very good gas mileage.

wheel

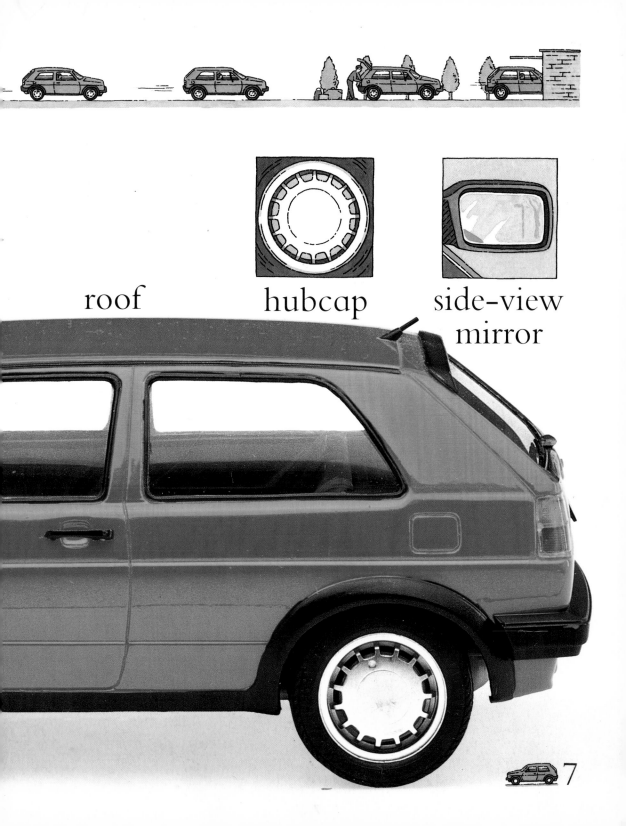

roof                   hubcap          side-view
                                         mirror

7

# Sedan

A sedan is a big car and usually has four doors. There is lots of room inside, so traveling is comfortable. Bags can be carried in the trunk. A sedan has a powerful engine that uses a lot of gasoline.

gas cap          headrest

trunk

# Convertible

Convertibles are fun to drive on warm, sunny days. When the top is down, you can feel the wind rushing by. If the weather turns bad, the top goes back up.

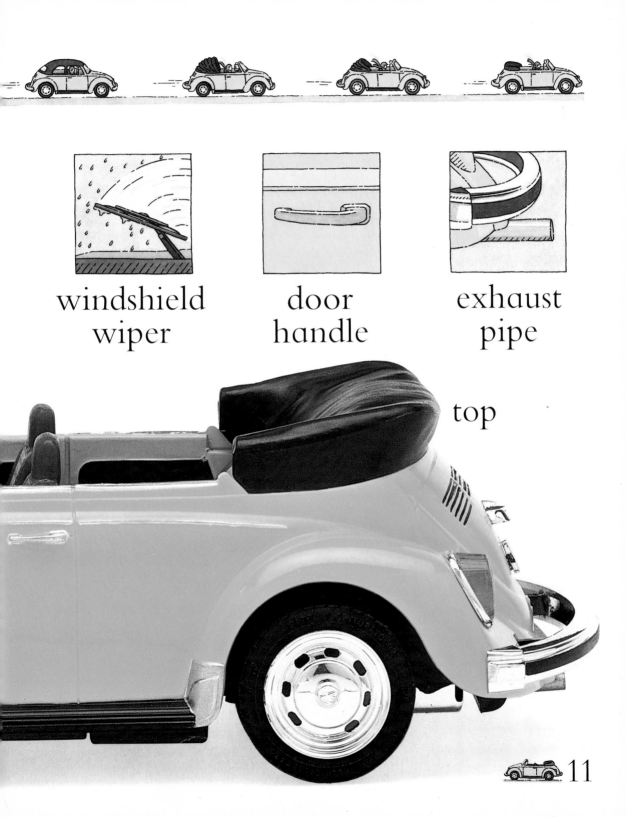

windshield
wiper

door
handle

exhaust
pipe

top

# Sports car

Sports cars are built to go very fast. A sleek shape helps them reach top speeds. Seats are close to the floor so the driver rides low. Sports cars zip past other cars on the road.

headlight

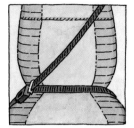
seat belt

trunk

wheel

# Racing car

Racing cars have powerful engines and are made for driving around a track. They ride super close to the ground and have big, wide tires. During long races the tires need to be changed. They wear out from going so fast!

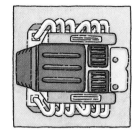

engine

tire

car body

# Vintage car

This car is very old. It was built many years ago when only a few people traveled by car. The owners had a chauffeur to drive them around. Today some people collect vintage cars.

hood

radiator
grill

mudguard

hood
ornament

# Jeep

This jeep can drive off the road, across muddy fields, or up steep hills. Its big wheels grip the ground and stop the car from sliding. Jeeps are strong and can pull heavy trailers.

bumper

steering
wheel

gas can

spare
tire

trailer
hitch

 19

# Police car

The police patrol the streets in cars like this. They have two-way radios to talk to the police station. When police cars drive fast, they use the flashing light and siren. This warns people to stay out of the way.

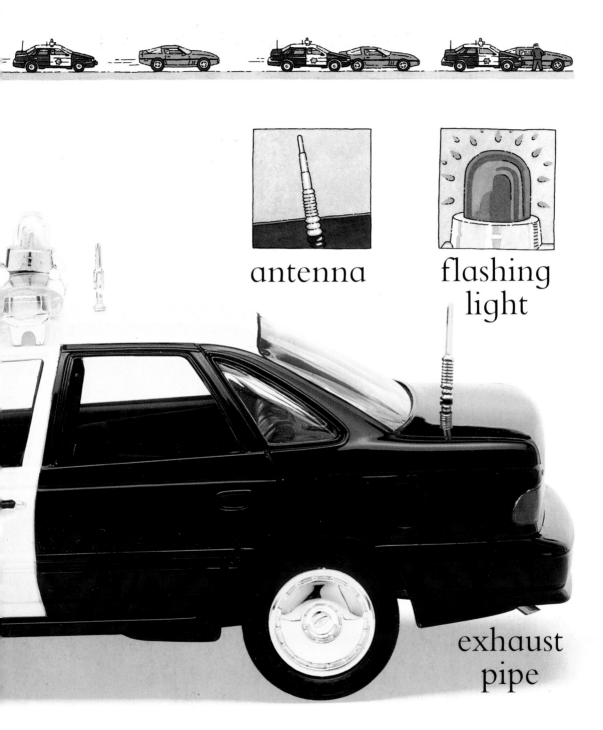

antenna

flashing
light

exhaust
pipe